RETURN TO THE LIBRARY OF DOOM

GHOST WRITER

BY MICHAEL DAHL

Illustrated by
Brad...

www.raintreepublishers.co.uk
Visit our website to find out
more information about
Raintree books.

To order:
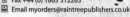 
☎ Phone 0845 6044371
▤ Fax +44 (0) 1865 312263
✉ Email myorders@raintreepublishers.co.uk

Customers from outside the UK please telephone +44 1865 312262

Raintree is an imprint of Capstone Global Library Limited, a company
incorporated in England and Wales having its registered office at 7 Pilgrim
Street, London, EC4V 6LB – Registered company number: 6695582

Text © Stone Arch Books 2012
First published in the United Kingdom in hardback and paperback by
Capstone Global Library Ltd in 2012
The moral rights of the proprietor have been asserted.

Art Director: Kay Fraser
Graphic Designer: Hilary Wacholz
Production Specialist: Michelle Biedscheid
Originated by Capstone Global Library Ltd
Printed in and bound in China by Leo Paper Products Ltd

ISBN 978 1 406 23699 6 (paperback)
15 14 13 12 11
10 9 8 7 6 5 4 3 2 1

British Library Cataloguing in Publication Data
A full catalogue record for this book is available from the British Library.

Contents

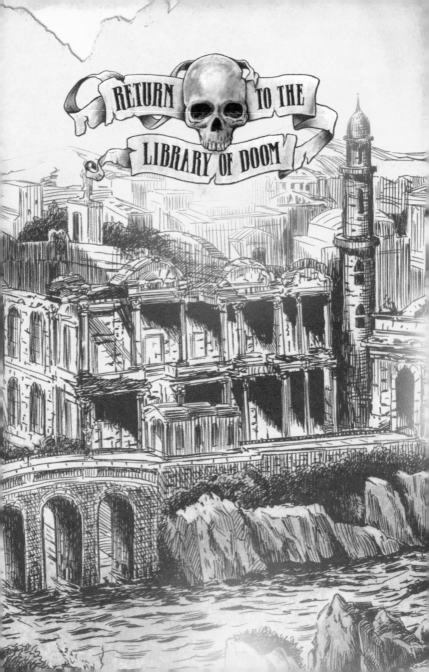

Behold the Library of Doom! The world's
largest collection of deadly and dangerous
books. Only the Librarian can prevent
these books from falling into the hands
of those who would use them for evil.

CAN A BOOK BE WRITTEN BY SOMEONE
WHO'S ALREADY DEAD . . . ?

Chapter 1

Simon Skull

Josh steps into the book shop and out of the pouring RAIN. He rushes up to the counter.

"Do you have any more books by Simon Skull?" Josh asks.

The young man behind the counter sneers. "Skull?" he says. "Why would you want to read that **rubbish**?"

"It's been years since Simon Skull wrote a new book," the man adds. "He's **disappeared** off the face of the Earth."

"I know," says Josh, **NODDING** sadly.

"His last book was *Seven Cold Fingers*.

"But I was hoping there were more.
Maybe there were some books I didn't
know about."

"Don't waste your time reading his
books," says the man. "There are a lot
of better writers out there. Besides, his
books will **ROT** your brain. He only
wrote about ghosts and zombies . . ."

" . . . and nameless creatures and **ALIEN** monsters," Josh adds. "I know! Isn't it great? Are you sure there aren't any more?"

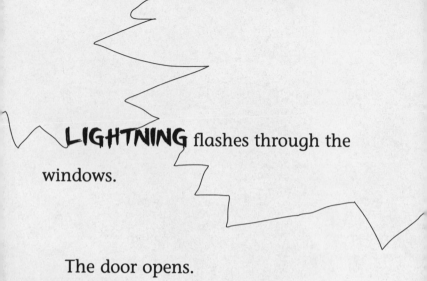

LIGHTNING flashes through the windows.

The door opens.

A woman stands in the doorway.

She has long **dark** hair. She wears a long coat over her clothes.

"Excuse me," says the woman. "Do you sell BLANK books?"

The bookseller looks DOWN at the counter.

"No. Sorry," he says. "No blank books."

The woman stares **hard** at the bookseller.

"Are there other book shops on this street?" she asks. "They must be WARNED."

"Warned?" asks the bookseller.

"There's one on the corner," says Josh.

Lightning flashes again and the woman is gone.

Chapter 2

Blank Book

Josh RUSHES out into the storm.

He races to the book shop on the corner.

What did that woman mean? he wonders.

Josh steps inside the second shop
and brushes the rain from his sleeves.

The book shop is **SILENT**. The
woman is not here.

"Hello?" calls Josh. No one answers.

There is no one behind the counter.

Maybe the owner is helping another customer, Josh thinks.

The bookstore is crammed full of TALL shelves and shadowy passages.

A dim lamp burns on the old counter.

Josh notices a package on the counter. The wrapping paper is torn open. A book lies inside.

He sees a small title stamped in
GOLD on the cover.

The book **RISES** a few inches into the air.

It falls back down onto the counter with a thump.

Josh steps back. Then he hears a soft SCRATCHING sound.

"Who's there?" croaks Josh. His throat is dry.

The scratching, crinkling sound
GROWS louder.

The brown wrapping paper on the
counter is moving.

It slowly crunches itself into a ball.

Josh stares in HORROR.

Then the paper unfolds itself and lies **FLAT** on the counter.

On the paper, Josh sees **words** that weren't there before.

Help me.

Chapter 3
The Second Package

Josh races back to the other book shop. He bursts through the door.

"HELP!" he shouts.

But the young man behind the counter is gone.

Josh's skin begins to **tingle**.

On the counter he sees a package.
Its wrapping paper is **torn** open too.

"Is anyone here?" shouts Josh.

The book shop is **SILENT**.

Nothing moves. The paper lies still.

Josh moves slowly towards the counter.

He wants to see if there is a book
inside this wrapping paper, too.

Josh steps behind the counter for a
closer look.

His shoe hits a book. Josh bends down
and picks it up.

It is a blank book.

Another one, Josh tells himself.

He places the book on the counter.

Then he carefully pokes the torn wrapping paper.

It doesn't move.

Josh *leans* closer to the paper.

A return address is **WRITTEN** on
one of the corners.

"Simon Skull!" shouts Josh.

Skull's address is written underneath his name.

"I don't believe it," Josh whispers.

Suddenly, the blank book floats above the counter. Then it **hurls** itself through the shop's window.

Chapter 4

The Milky Eye

Lightning **crackles** above the city streets.

As Josh runs towards King Street, he sees a shadow ahead.

The dark shape reminds him of the **STRANGE** woman back at the book shop.

She was looking for blank books, thinks Josh.

Several minutes later, Josh finds the address.

It is an old, **CRUMBLING** building.

A doorman in a faded uniform stands outside.

The man is all skin and **BONES**.

He smiles at Josh.

As Josh nears the building, the doorman leans towards him. He has one green eye and one that's white as milk.

The doorman stares at Josh.

He opens the **HEAVY** door and Josh
steps inside.

A list of names covers the wall of
the narrow entrance.

Beside each name is the flat number.

\#

\#

\#

Josh runs his finger down the list.

"There's no **SKULL** anywhere," he says.

Then he looks for Flat 13.

Next to the number is the name:

HARRY GIBBON

Josh **frowns**.

Could that be his real name? Josh wonders. *Maybe he uses a fake name so people won't bother him.*

Josh puts his hands in his jacket pockets. *I wonder if he'll think I'm bothering him.*

But I'm his **biggest** fan, thinks Josh.

I just want to tell him how great he is.

How he needs to write another book.

That wouldn't be bothering him,

would it? Josh is not sure.

The outside door opens with a

LOUD sucking sound. The doorman

sticks his head inside.

"You know where you're going?" he asks Josh.

His milky eye **gleams** in the dim light.

"Sure, sure," says Josh. "I just wanted to **dry** off before I went upstairs."

The doorman slowly nods his head. Josh steps into the huge, **DARK** entrance hall.

His **wet** shoes squeak against the smooth marble floor.

"Are you sure you know where you're going?" repeats the doorman.

"I'm going upstairs now," says Josh.

He puts his hand on the cool stone hand rail and CLIMBS the stairs.

Chapter 5

Flat 13

Josh hears something scratching in the hallways.

Rats?

The sound reminds him of the wrapping paper that **crunched** itself into a ball.

The sound GROWS louder as Josh nears a door at the end of a hallway.

It is Flat 13.

The door is partly open.

Josh hears the SCRATCHING sound. It's coming from inside the flat.

He also hears a woman's voice.

"Scribble, scribble, scribble,
Mr Gibbon?"

Josh recognizes the voice.

As he steps into the flat, he sees the
strange woman from the book shop.

She is speaking to a man sitting at a desk. His face and hands are hidden in shadow.

The man holds a pen in his right hand. He is WRITING in a blank book.

A stack of blank books sits next to him on the FLOOR.

"You must **stop** this," says the woman.

The man looks up at her.

"I thought you liked books," he says. "You like lots and lots of **BOOKS**. Here. Have this one!"

He **throws** a book into her hands. As soon as her fingers touch the blank book, the woman begins to FADE.

HA!   HA!

The man **laughs**.   *HA!*

        HA!

"All those people who hated my

Simon Skull books – they said I was

nothing! Said I was just a blank!" shouts

the man. "Well, now they're all blank!

Everyone who touches these books turns

into a big, **fat** nothing. A zero! A

ghost!"

Josh stares in horror.

The blank book **hovers** above

the floor.

The woman must still be holding it, he

thinks. *She's still there, but she's not there.*

A ghost.

Chapter 6

Gibbon and Skull

Josh feels the HAIR on the back of his neck standing up.

The shadowy man turns and stares.

"You!" cries the man. "Who are you?"

Josh's throat feels **DRY**.

"Uh . . . uh . . ." he croaks. "I'm just a fan . . ."

A hand **grips** his shoulder.

Josh looks up and sees a man standing behind him.

The man is **TALL**. He wears a long black coat and dark glasses.

The man looks down at Josh and smiles. "I think," he says, "that **Mr Gibbon** was talking to me."

The shadowy writer **JUMPS** up from his chair.

"You're the Librarian," he says.

The **DARK** stranger nods.

"And you have my blank books," the Librarian says. "And my friend."

The Librarian raises his arm and points to the blank book, still floating in mid-air. It **flies** into his hand.

The Librarian pulls a pen from his pocket. He **crosses** out the word that the Skull had written.

Then he writes another word:
SKYWRITER.

The woman reappears in the middle of the room.

She looks at the Librarian. "Thanks," she says.

Josh notices something. The shadowy author has **VANISHED**. "Simon Skull!" cries Josh. "He's gone!"

Josh looks up at the two **strangers**. "You have to find him. You have to stop him!"

The Librarian looks grim. "Don't worry. That was only his shadow," he says.

He nods towards another door in the flat. Josh peeks into the room.

A body is lying on a **dirty** bed.

"It's Skull," says Skywriter. "Or Gibbon. Whatever his real name is. And he's been there for quite some time."

Slowly, Josh ENTERS the room.

He sees the man's head **lying** on the pillow.

The man does not move. The man does not breathe.

His eyes stare at the ceiling. One green eye and one as white as milk.

Author

Michael Dahl is the author of more than 200 books for children and young adults. He has won the AEP Distinguished Achievement Award three times for his non-fiction. His Finnegan Zwake mystery series was shortlisted twice by the Anthony and Agatha awards. He has also written the Dragonblood series. He is a featured speaker at conferences on graphic novels and high-interest books for boys.

Illustrator

Bradford Kendall has enjoyed drawing for as long as he can remember. As a boy, he loved to read comic books and watch old monster films. He graduated from university with a BFA in Illustration. He has owned his own commercial art business since 1983, and lives with his wife, Leigh, and their two children, Lily and Stephen. They also have a cat named Hansel and a dog named Gretel.

Glossary

alien creature from another planet

creature living being

disappear go out of sight

doorman person who works at a block of flats and lets people in or out

grim gloomy, stern, or unpleasant

horror great fear, terror, or shock

nameless having no name

recognize see or hear someone and know who the person is

return address address of the person who sent a letter or package, written so that the mail can be returned to them if necessary

sneer smile in a hateful, mocking way

warn tell a person about a danger or something that might happen

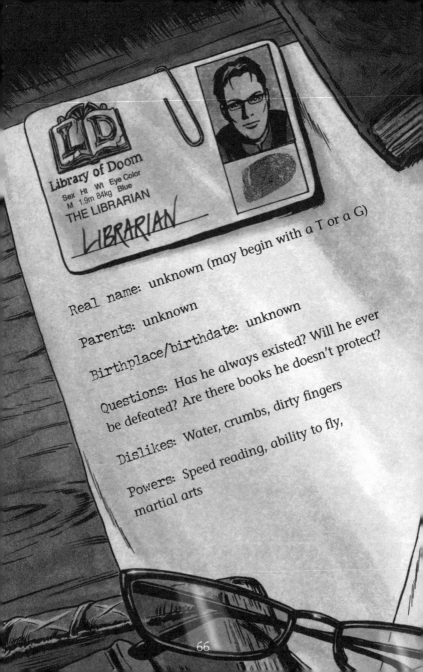

Library of Doom

Sex | Ht | Wt | Eye Color
M | 1.9m | 84kg | Blue

THE LIBRARIAN

LIBRARIAN

Real name: unknown (may begin with a T or a G)

Parents: unknown

Birthplace/birthdate: unknown

Questions: Has he always existed? Will he ever be defeated? Are there books he doesn't protect?

Dislikes: Water, crumbs, dirty fingers

Powers: Speed reading, ability to fly, martial arts

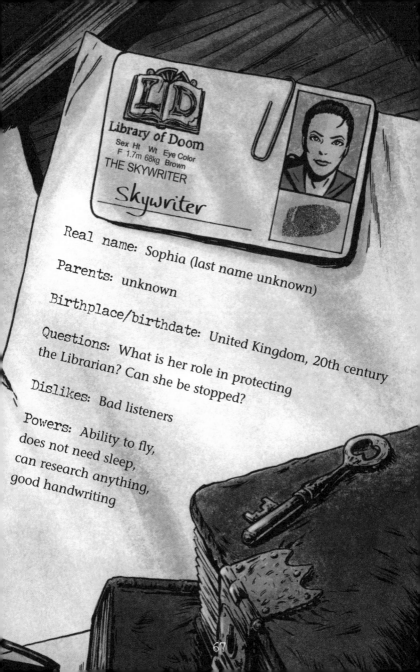

Library of Doom

Sex Ht Wt Eye Color
F 1.7m 68kg Brown

THE SKYWRITER

Skywriter

Real name: Sophia (last name unknown)

Parents: unknown

Birthplace/birthdate: United Kingdom, 20th century

Questions: What is her role in protecting the Librarian? Can she be stopped?

Dislikes: Bad listeners

Powers: Ability to fly, does not need sleep, can research anything, good handwriting

Simon Skull

After the Librarian defeated it, Harry Gibbon's shadow retreated to wherever shadows go. But the legend of Gibbon himself lives on.

Though his books, written under the pen name Simon Skull, were all bestsellers, many critics said that he could tell a great story, but that he wasn't a good writer. Gibbon, who had received a PhD in English, hated hearing those comments. He became stranger and stranger, eventually refusing to leave his tiny apartment for months at a time.

Eventually, it seems, Harry Gibbon got his revenge. But the Librarian — who prefers a good story to perfect grammar any time — had to defeat Harry Gibbon's shadow, for fear he'd make more books blank.

DISCUSSION QUESTIONS

1. What happened to Harry Gibbon/Simon Skull?

2. Do you know the difference between a good story and a well-written story? Which do you prefer to read? Talk about it.

3. Josh wants to tell SIMON SKULL that Skull is his favourite author. But he worries that it would be bothering Mr Skull. What do you think? Is it impolite to tell a well-known person your opinion of his or her work?

WRITING PROMPTS

1. Make your own BLANK BOOK using paper and a stapler. Fill it with whatever you want!

2. Try writing this story from Harry Gibbon/Simon Skull's point of view. What does he think? What does he see? How does he feel?

3. Who's your **FAVOURITE** author? Write a letter to that person.

More books from the Library of Doom

Return to the Library of Doom